The Ghost Fox

The Ghost Fox

BY LAURENCE YEP

ILLUSTRATED BY

JEAN AND MOU-SIEN TSENG

A
LITTLE APPLE
PAPERBACK

SCHOLASTIC INC.
New York Toronto London Auckland Sydney

ISBN 0-590-47205-4

12 11 10 9 8 7 6 5 4 3 2 1   2   6 7 8 9/9 0 1/0

Printed in the U.S.A.   40

Book design by Claire Counihan

To my uncle,

TOMMY KIM,

who said I ought to learn some

of the old stories

— L.Y.

Contents

The Ghost Fox

1. Wind to the Sea

THE TRADERS of Hunan sail their flatboats far down the Great River to the sea itself. One of the boldest traders was Big Lee, and his son was called Little Lee, and they lived in a crescent-shaped town on a bend of the Great River.

Early one spring, Big Lee put on his traveling coat. Outside it was embroidered blue felt, and inside it was warm fleecy wool. "The winds are blowing me and mine to the sea," he announced.

From the storerooms he took his treasures. There were lumps of gold and silver for the smiths, rare woods for the carpenters, and teas and perfumes for the merchants. For the gardeners he had yellow lotuses from the high mountain streams. To the collectors he would sell strange stones that looked like polished black clouds full of holes.

Though he was only nine, Little Lee helped his father and crew take the baskets down the winding dirt street to the river docks. They passed houses whose window frames were filled with little panes of polished oyster shell. Their windows looked like soft, milky spiders' eyes.

Little Lee followed his father and the crew. He carried a stack of boxes taller than himself, so he could not see where he was going. He kept bumping into the walls of the houses on the street. Finally, he brushed against a young gentleman in a red robe. "Watch it, you clumsy little fool!" The gentleman raised a hand to hit Little Lee.

Little Lee tried to hide behind his boxes, but Big Lee dropped his burden. "Hey!" he

shouted and caught the gentleman's wrist. "My boy didn't mean any harm. If he's damaged your robe, we'll pay for it. But don't hit him."

The gentleman glared at Big Lee. "How dare you touch me!"

"I'm so sorry," Big Lee laughed. He let go of the gentleman by shoving him backward. The young gentleman plopped down in the dirt.

Angrily the young gentleman jumped to his feet. "You're not sorry now, but you will be."

"I'm ready," Big Lee said and raised his fists for a fight.

The gentleman, however, straightened up and dusted himself off. "Only common folk brawl in the street. I have my own ways of getting even." Quickly he hurried off before Big Lee could grab him.

Big Lee helped Little Lee pick up his boxes again. "I'm sorry, Father."

Big Lee just laughed. "Those kind of fellows always talk big and do nothing."

Together, they spent the rest of the day filling up Big Lee's boat with treasures. They stopped only when the boat was so heavy that its deck rode only inches from the dark, chocolate water.

Then Big Lee took one last look at his home. The green-tiled roofs swept down the slopes to the water like even piles of leaves.

Little Lee's mother had come to the wharf to say good-bye. "Come back soon."

Lifting up his son, Big Lee gave him a big hug and said, "I'll be home in time for the New Year—even if the river dries up and I have to walk back." And he set his son down on the dock.

Little Lee let loose the line and stood with his mother. On the boat, Big Lee and his crew raised their sails. The wind blew across the river and swept Big Lee's boat toward the big sea. Little Lee stayed on the dock until the boat was lost to view.

2. Prowlers

WHEN Little Lee and his mother reluctantly started back home, Little Lee saw the gentleman in the red robe. The man smiled slyly and rubbed his narrow chin.

As he and his mother trudged up the hill, Little Lee glanced behind him. Sure enough, Red Robe was trailing them in the crowded, winding street. He always kept a careful distance. Red Robe slowed down if they slowed down. He hurried when they hurried so that he did not lose sight of them.

Their house sat upon the brow of the hill, shoulder to shoulder with the homes of their neighbors. When they stopped at their front door, Little Lee tugged at his mother's robe. "I think someone followed us home."

"Really?" His mother turned to look, but the man had vanished.

Little Lee scratched his head. "He was just here." Little Lee searched all around the crowded street, but he saw no one.

That night, as a precaution, his mother went to the front door and bolted it. Then she went to the back door and bolted it as well.

"Now," she declared to Little Lee, "if anyone tries to come in, you and I are safe."

Later that night, a scrabbling sound woke Little Lee. It sounded as if an animal was outside their house. It sounded as if claws were scraping the hard dirt outside.

Little Lee lay under his quilt, listening. Now he heard a rattling. He thought some creature was trying to open the front door.

Little Lee had a tiny window that looked out on the street. It was small so that the family luck would not leak out. Moonlight

slipped through the panes of polished shells. It cast a soft, glowing pool of light on the floor. Little Lee thought he saw the shadow of a fox against the window.

"Who's there?" he asked sharply.

Instantly the shadow vanished. After a moment he heard his mother's soft footsteps as she came to his door. Opening it, she peered inside. "Are you all right, dear?"

Little Lee pointed toward the street. "Mama, I saw a fox."

"They usually don't come into town," his mother said. "Let's check."

Hand in hand, they made their way through the dark house to the front door. Mama slid the bar back and opened the door. Outside, the street was deserted.

Little Lee squatted down, but there were too many footprints and tracks in the dirt. He could barely distinguish one human footprint from another. "I could have sworn it was a fox."

"You must have heard rats," Mama said. She barred the front door once again.

"Tomorrow we'll put some poison out."

Even so, Little Lee made her check the back door. He felt better when he saw that it was also barred, and he let his mother take him back to his room. "Mama, are foxes dangerous?" Little Lee asked as he lay down on his mat.

She smiled and pulled the quilt about his neck. "You're bigger than they are."

Little Lee looked up at her. "Father says they can steal people's souls."

She sat down beside him. "You're safe here."

"But, Mama—"

"Hush." She began to hum the lullaby "By the Gate."

Little Lee recognized the tune. "You used to sing that all the time when I was small."

His mother smiled and caressed his forehead. "That's because you would never take a nap."

In the dim light, her face began to blur. She was still humming when Little Lee fell asleep.

3. Floating Villages

THE NEXT DAY, Little Lee went to school, and his mother went out to buy rat poison. When Little Lee came home, she showed him where she had stored the jar on a high shelf. "I don't want you to go near it," Mama warned him.

When Little Lee had promised, she held out her hand. "Come. Let's go look for your father."

Together, they walked down the winding street to the busy docks. Standing off to one side, they searched the big, broad river. There were no sails, but they saw thatched roofs sweeping down toward them.

"I see a whole village coming toward us, Mama," Little Lee said.

His mother laughed. "The woodsmen make a giant raft out of their pine logs and build a village on top of it. Then they sail down the river to one of the great cities, where they break up the raft and village and sell the lumber. In the meantime the woodsmen live in huts with their families."

By now the floating village was right in front of them. The shacks stood in a circle on the giant raft. They had roofs of straw and walls of pine branches. Smoke rose from fires on flat stones where families were cooking.

On the bow a man kept watch for rocks and shallows. Other men stood on the port and starboard sides with poles, ready to shove the raft away from trouble.

A curtain of faded green cloth flapped, and a boy about Little Lee's age stepped outside. He brought a cup of tea to the man at the bow. "Here, Father," they heard him say.

The man took it and nodded his thanks. Then, standing side by side, they kept watch together.

As the raft floated past, Little Lee felt envious. "If Father traveled on a raft, we could go with him," he said.

"Wouldn't that be nice?" Mama said wistfully. "But at least you and I have each other. Poor Father has no one but his crew; and they're not really family."

Little Lee patted her hand. "One day I'll be old enough to go with Father. Then what will you do, Mama?"

"Go with you," Little Lee's mother said, "but you're going to be my little boy for a long time."

Suddenly Little Lee saw the gentleman in the red robe. "Mama, that's him!"

By the time his mother turned around, the man had slipped away in the crowd.

"We'd better go back," she said. Mama took Little Lee by the hand and they quickly returned home.

After that, Little Lee and his mother

would go down to the docks every day after school. They stood for a long time by the river, straining their eyes as they tried to catch a glimpse of Big Lee's boat.

Sometimes, though, Little Lee thought he saw the gentleman in the red robe; but when he looked again, Red Robe was gone. Some nights, he heard the scrabbling noise on the roof. The doors and windows rattled as if something was trying to get in.

Though they put out poison every day, Little Lee and his mother never caught any rats.

4. Winter

SPRING LED to summer, and summer led to fall. Still, Big Lee did not return home.

Winter came especially cold and harsh. The sky was dark with clouds. Snow covered the streets and rooftops. Yet, as the time for New Year's approached, little buds like green fur began to appear on the bare branches of the plum tree in the courtyard. "Father will be home any day now," Little Lee said. Even in the snow, he insisted on walking down to the river to greet his father.

Wearing their padded coats, Little Lee and his mother shuffled through the slippery streets until they reached the docks. There were no boats in sight. Rocks stuck out of the water sharp as fangs. Sandy shoals twisted as if they were giant yellow snakes.

Mama sighed when she saw how low the water was. "You know," she hinted to Little Lee, "your father might not be able to keep his promise. Don't be disappointed if he's not home in time for the New Year."

Little Lee refused to believe his mother. "Father always keeps his word."

They both felt very sad as they made their way up the hill and back home.

That night Mama made dinner silently. It was Little Lee's job to feed bundles of reeds into the rectangular openings in the front of the brick stove. While he kept the fire going, he usually told his mother all about school. However, that night Little Lee didn't feel like talking, either.

Nor did his mother speak while they ate. After supper, Mama sighed. "I'm sorry that I'm not good company tonight."

Little Lee patted her hand. "It's all right,

Mama. I feel sad, too. I thought Papa would be home for the New Year."

His mother smiled gently. "I just want to sleep and forget about how sad I feel."

Little Lee nodded his head in understanding. "Maybe we'll dream of Father."

"That's just the thing to cheer me up," his mother agreed and rose from the table. "Let's forget about chores tonight and go to bed instead. And when we awake tomorrow, we'll be our old selves."

So they did just that. They didn't even clean the dishes.

However, sleep brought neither peace nor dreams of his father. Little Lee tossed and turned restlessly. Suddenly he heard his mother cry out, "Help!"

Instantly, Little Lee shot up from the mat. Calling to his mother, he burst out of his room and skidded into the living room.

In the darkness, the furniture looked like monstrous hulks, and he halted in fear. As his eyes adjusted to the dim starlight, he saw that the back door stood open. His mother and he had been in too much of a hurry to go to sleep. The one chore they had neglected was to check the doors.

Little Lee kept bumping into things until he reached the door. Behind him, he heard a funny scratching sound of claws on the floor. Then something small and furry shot past him.

"Darn those rats," Little Lee said and slammed the door shut. He groped blindly along the wall until he found the bolt and slid it home.

When the rear door was safely secured, he went to his mother's room. Mama was sitting on her mat, her hair all tangled and matted. When he stepped through the doorway, her head jerked up and she stared at him with wide eyes as if she did not recognize him.

Little Lee stood uncertainly. "Mama, are you all right?"

His mother blinked her eyes. "Thank Heaven!" Rising from her mat, she swept him into her arms and hugged him tightly.

"Mama," he wheezed. "I can't breathe."

His mother sat down as rigidly as ever and did not loosen her grip. "Mama, you look so strange. What's wrong?" Little Lee asked.

She clung to him as if she would never let go. "I feel as if I were drowning in an invisible river," she said. "Don't desert me."

"I won't," Little Lee promised, "even if I have to go to the bottom of the river to find you."

His mother let out her breath raggedly in a frightened sigh. "I'm depending on you." Finally she let him go.

With his fingers, he began to comb her hair. "I thought I saw a rat inside the house."

"As if we didn't have enough troubles." His mother tried to smile. "Fetch my brush."

As Little Lee got it from her bureau, she lit a candle. Quickly she brushed her hair before a bronze mirror.

Then they went outside together. The light from the candle cast strange shadows around the house. As they moved, the shadows twisted and writhed.

As frightened as Little Lee, Mama moved slowly to the pantry where she took out the poison. She seemed to feel a little better after she had set it out all around the house.

"I don't think I can sleep tonight," Mama said.

"That's all right. Then don't," Little Lee comforted her.

Returning to the pantry, they took out all the other candles and brought them to her room. When they were lit, the room was as bright as day. They played games and told one another stories until the sun rose.

5. A Cry in the Night

IN THE MORNING, Little Lee's mother kept him home from school because she felt so nervous and afraid. That evening she even moved Little Lee's mat into her room. "It's silly, I know, but I want you to sleep in here tonight." And when they lay down, she left the candle lit.

Little Lee was determined to stay awake that night. Once his mother was asleep, he sat up, leaning against the wall. In his head he did sums, but toward midnight he nodded off.

The gentleman in the red robe haunted

his sleep. After one awful nightmare, Little Lee woke with a start. "Mama, I had the strangest dream," he said.

Horrified, he saw that his mother's sleeping mat was empty.

"Mama?" he called. "Mama?"

Taking the big red candle in his hand, he stepped outside. A breeze almost blew out the candle flame. Quickly, he lifted his free hand to protect the fragile light.

It was easy to trace the draft to a broken window frame. Anxiously, he searched the house. His mother was in the kitchen, perched on top of the stove. She lay curled up on her side. Her head rested on her hands.

"Mama?" He put his hand on her shoulder and shook her until her eyelids opened.

"What are you doing in the kitchen?" she asked.

"What are you doing here?" Little Lee asked.

His mother stretched and yawned elabo-

rately. "I don't know. I must have walked in my sleep."

Little Lee tried to help his mother from the stove, but she slid off on her own. He followed his mother to her bedroom, where she lay down and quickly went back to sleep. Again, Little Lee fought to stay awake. He knew something strange was happening, but he fell asleep right away.

The next morning, his mother woke him. "No more loafing around," she told him. "Today you go to school."

"But yesterday you wanted me to stay home," Little Lee protested.

His mother smiled crookedly. "Why would I do a silly thing like that? I'm feeling perfectly fine."

Puzzled, Little Lee obeyed her and went to school.

That afternoon, Little Lee carefully checked the front of their house. The window frame had not been repaired. It was odd. His parents did not neglect their house like that.

Opening the front door, he looked inside anxiously. "Mama?"

"In here," she called from the kitchen.

When Little Lee found her, she was sitting on the table in her best gown. "Do you want me to get Big Hands?" Big Hands was a carpenter who sometimes did work for them. "He can fix the window frame."

Mama overturned her small jewelry chest so that everything poured out next to her. "I don't care if it's broken. This house was getting too stuffy," she sniffed. "We need some air in here."

Little Lee took a piece of steamed bread from a plate. Though it was stale, he ate it. "Shall we go down to the river?" he asked. "Maybe we'll be able to see Father today."

Mama put on all her jewelry: rings, necklaces, and bracelets. "There will be nothing to see but water and more water. He'll come when he'll come."

Little Lee began to protest, "But, Mama—"

With a frown, she flicked a necklace at

him. "Stop being so tiresome." No matter
how he pleaded, she refused to take him
down to the docks.

Disappointed, Little Lee went to his room
and found that his mother had moved his
mat back from her room.

Returning to the kitchen, he asked her,
"Why did you move my mat?"

His mother laughed as she studied herself
in the mirror of her small jewelry chest.
"You've been acting very silly lately. You
have your own bedroom."

"But it was your idea!" Little Lee argued.

"Now why would I do any such thing? I'm
not the foolish one. You are." When his
mother raised her arms, all of her bracelets
jangled loudly. "Now go next door to Auntie Spring and ask her if she can spare something for supper."

When he returned, Little Lee sulkily set
the leftovers in front of his mother. She did
not seem very concerned. In fact, she ignored him while they ate their meal.

As he gathered up the dirty dishes after

supper, she told him to leave them. "Go to bed."

"But I have a test tomorrow," he said. "I have to study."

"Don't be such a little drudge. You know enough boring facts already." She shoved him toward his bedroom.

Little Lee stared at her. She looked like his mother. She sounded like her. But she didn't act at all like Mama.

"Go to bed." She gave him another shove.

Though Little Lee went to his room and lay down on his mat, he did not go to sleep. "Mama ordered me to go to bed," he said to himself. "She didn't say I had to go to sleep."

He rested on his side and stared at his window. For hours, he tried to think of a way to send a message to his father. Something was wrong with Mama.

The trouble was that it was winter. There were no boats on the river. No travelers on the roads. Little Lee thought and thought, but he could come up with no solution.

In the middle of the night he heard the scrabbling sound again. He listened carefully until he was sure it came from inside the house and not outside on the street.

"Mama," he called, "I think the rats are inside the house again."

His mother did not reply. Moonlight spilled through the broken window frame. Why didn't she have it fixed? Little Lee wondered.

Suddenly he heard a high, wild shriek from his mother's bedroom.

Stumbling through the dark, he raced to her bedroom. "Mama, are you all right?" he asked and knocked on her door.

His mother jerked the door open. In the light cast by the candle in her room, she looked pale and her hair flew out in all directions. "Shut up, you little pest. Quit making so much noise."

Little Lee stared up in surprise. His mother had never spoken so harshly to him. "Mama, are you okay?"

"Nothing that sleep couldn't cure." She

pointed toward his room. "Go back to bed."

Little Lee refused to go. "You're acting awfully funny lately."

Her eyes grew wider and wider. "You heard me. Go."

"Mama—"

She pushed him out of her room. "You obey me."

"But, Mama—" he tried to protest.

"Behave, or else," she snapped, and slammed her door shut.

Little Lee returned sadly to his room. He was certain that someone had cast a spell over Mama. Maybe the evil was entering through the broken window. He would repair it tomorrow.

6. *Home Repair*

THE NEXT MORNING, Little Lee could do nothing right. From the moment he woke up, his mother cursed him and said terrible things.

Little Lee covered his ears and said to himself, "This is not my mother. This is some stranger."

And yet his mother was all kind smiles when she talked to her neighbors. None of them suspected a thing.

Little Lee felt like running away to find Father. Then he remembered that he had promised not to leave his mother. He said to himself, "I must save Mama somehow."

So he did not go to school. He knew he had to repair the window, but he could not ask his mother for help. If she was already under someone's evil spell, she would not want anyone to fix the window. Little Lee would have to get what he needed from their neighbor, Auntie Spring.

First, though, he went down to the riverbank. He gathered stones and put them into an old basket. Then he lugged them up the slope back home.

Auntie Spring was in her doorway, sweeping the dust out of her house. When she saw Little Lee panting with his basket, she stopped. "Why aren't you in school?" she asked suspiciously. "And what are you doing with all those stones? You're not going to throw them, are you?"

Little Lee had already planned his story. "I'm fixing the house," he declared. Setting the basket down, he tipped it on its side. All the rocks rolled out with a clatter.

When his mother heard the noise, she

came outside. "You should be in school."

She stood in his way, but Little Lee protested. "I promised Father that I would take care of the house."

"Your father would want you to go to school," Auntie Spring scolded.

"I need to fix the window first," Little Lee insisted.

"That's just an excuse, you lazy thing," Auntie Spring grumbled. "You don't want to study."

Little Lee ignored her as he gathered his rocks into a pile beneath the broken window. Though Auntie Spring clucked her tongue, Little Lee pretended that he didn't care.

"Let the boy get a taste of real work," Auntie Spring advised his mother. "Eventually he'll get tired and be grateful to return to his books."

As Little Lee suspected, his mother pretended she was still her kind old self. "Don't let him annoy you." But she leaned over Little Lee as he worked. "You'll be sorry," she whispered again. Then she went back inside.

By late afternoon, Little Lee had made several trips to the river, collecting stones. Then he went to Auntie Spring's house and asked her for a pot of hot water and a bench. He needed the hot water so that he could make mud, and the bench so that he could reach the window.

"Still at it?" Auntie Spring asked. "I thought the hard work and the cold would have gotten to you by now."

"When I start a job, I finish it, Auntie," he grinned.

To humor him, Auntie Spring gave him what he wanted. After making mud with the hot water, he began to set his stones on the windowsill. As soon as he had one layer down, he slapped a handful of steaming mud on top. When it froze, the mud would be harder than any cement.

By the end of the day, Little Lee had filled both windows with stones and carefully stuffed all the spaces with mud.

Satisfied, he returned the pot and bench to Auntie Spring. When she saw the sweaty, mud-covered boy, she sighed. "You're not usually such a willful child. Have you lost your senses? Only a senseless person would work this long in the snow. Heaven help your poor mother."

"Yes," Little Lee agreed. "Heaven help her."

7. *The Guardian*

WHEN Little Lee went home, his mother sent him back to Auntie Spring to borrow supper. "Why don't you just borrow my whole house?" she grumbled.

"My mother isn't herself," Little Lee explained, "so she doesn't feel like cooking."

"It's her wretched son who's made her feel poorly." Auntie Spring got some food. "I'm doing this for your poor mother. Not for you. You're a lazy boy."

When he returned, his mother served just herself. "You have to learn to obey me. So tonight, you will go without supper." She popped a tender piece of beef into her mouth. She began to chew, smiling at the taste.

Little Lee's empty belly began to growl with hunger, but he went to his room. He was so tired, but he did not dare lie down. Instead, he changed into clean clothes and waited. To keep awake, he remembered all the good times he had shared with Mama. He wanted those days to return.

At midnight, he heard the scrabbling noise outside his room. When the house was silent again, he opened his door and peered out. All was dark inside the house.

Quickly he lit a candle in his room. Then he tiptoed to the front door. As he had suspected, his mother had left it unbolted. He slid the wooden bolt home. Fetching the sharpest knife he could find from the kitchen, he hurried to his mother's door and shouted, "Fire!"

Instantly the door banged open, and a small, furry red fox shot by. Little Lee swung but missed. Thinking he had trapped the

creature, he chased it. However, when the fox reached the front door, the wooden bolt snapped as if it were a toothpick. Little Lee watched in amazement as the door magically swung open.

As the fox darted out into the street, Little Lee chopped at it. When he held up his candle, he saw about two inches of red bushy tail and drops of blood on the snow.

His mother snatched up the bit of tail and then yanked the knife and candle from his hands. "Get out!" she screamed. Shoving him into the street, she slammed the door.

"Help," Little Lee shouted.

Up and down the street, candles and lanterns and lamps were lit. As the neighbors stepped into the street, Little Lee appealed to them. "A ghost fox has cast a spell on my mother. I tried to catch it, but it got away. Look, you can see its blood."

However, the neighbors had trampled the snow all around his house and there were no longer any tracks or drops of blood.

"I swear it's the truth," Little Lee insisted.

Auntie Spring whispered loudly. "He's lost his senses. His poor mother's a saint to put up with him."

Though Little Lee begged them for help, they all turned their backs on him and instead returned to their homes. As he stood there alone in the snow, he knew then that only he could save his mother.

8. The Hunter

ALONE, Little Lee searched the streets for some sign of the ghost fox. Further up the block, he again found the drops of blood in the snow. He called out excitedly to the neighbors, but they remained indoors.

Refusing to be discouraged, Little Lee followed the trail. On either side, the snow-covered houses looked like fleecy sheep huddling for warmth. Reed fires cast a soft red glow on the oyster-shell windows.

Little Lee shivered as he tramped past the houses. He knew that inside, the villagers were warm and cozy. Cold and tired, he crossed the bridge over the canal. He was now in the older part of town.

Ahead he saw a glow on top of the hill. He forgot the cold. He forgot his hunger. The drops of blood led straight to the remains of the old Ho family mansion. It had once belonged to a famous family of traders.

Now the gates hung half off their hinges. Sun and wind had worn the paint off the old wood and reduced the carvings to worm tracks.

In the courtyard some stubborn weeds still thrust their way above the snow. Beyond the courtyard lay the roofless mansion. As with their home, the Ho family fortunes had been ruined long ago.

Suddenly he saw a flicker of light. A stream of stars danced through the front doorway. The next second, it vanished. Holding his breath, Little Lee slipped between the broken gates and across the courtyard.

Under the moon, he crept from room to room. From the rear of the house, shim-

mering ribbons of light slithered through the snowy rooms. Quietly, the boy followed the streamers of light. Finally, he came to a crumbling wall with an empty window frame. He crawled to the windowsill, rising just high enough to look into the garden. Most of the bushes and trees lay bare as skeletons. However, a half-dozen plum trees were just coming into blossom. The whiteness of the trees matched the whiteness of the ground.

Suddenly sparks of light shot into the sky and hovered in the air. More and more sparks rose until they formed long veils of light that trailed out in all directions and into the house.

Under the plum trees sat two men. One of them wore an elegant red robe. It was the man who had followed Little Lee home. The other man wore a brown robe and tended Red Robe. Little Lee guessed that Brown Robe must be a servant.

Brown Robe held a brush in his right hand. "There you are, sir," Brown Robe announced. "It's clean of blood and almost as bushy as ever."

The mysterious light flickered around them and dissolved into sparks.

Red Robe looked indignantly over his shoulder. "The wound is bad enough," Red Robe sniffed. "But to use a common kitchen knife. As if I were a cucumber." He raised a long fox's tail from the snow. It was as red as his robe—except at the tip. A bandage had been carefully tied there.

As the servant leaned forward to fuss over his master's tail, the hem of his brown robe twitched and a bushy fox's tail sprang free. It waved in the air for a moment before the servant tucked it away. "Some of these human kits are too frisky to know their place. But you'll fix him soon enough."

"He's young and small, so it shouldn't take as long to steal his soul." Red Robe carefully stowed his tail back under his clothing.

Brown Robe laughed harshly. "When will you finish stealing the mother's?"

"By tomorrow night, I'll have hers." Red

Robe plucked a plum blossom and smelled it.

Brown Robe hid the brush in his sleeve. "Then you'll want to celebrate."

Red Robe rubbed his chin. "I haven't had sweets in a long time."

"You have to keep your figure, sir," Brown Robe insisted. "What if I steal some nice turnips instead?"

"Fool, you don't celebrate a great victory with turnips." Red Robe rapped his servant on the head. "Bring me candy. I can go back on my diet after that."

Brown Robe sighed. "I'll try, sir. But the candy seller watches me all the time. The farmers never guard their turnips in the market."

Rapping Brown Robe on the skull again, Red Robe stalked off, holding his wounded tail in the air. Shaking his head, Brown Robe followed.

Little Lee watched the two ghost foxes disappear through a hole into another part of the ruined house.

9. The Quest

ONCE the ghost foxes left, Little Lee realized how cold he was. He huddled against the wall, trying to think of what to do. No one would believe him. Even if he could find his father, it would be too late to save Mama's soul.

Maybe if he could show everyone that Brown Robe had a fox's tail, he could convince them that Mama needed help. He knew that everything depended on him. Up until now, the grown-ups had only made mistakes.

Little Lee thought and thought. If a ghost

fox could pass as a human, perhaps a human could pass as a ghost fox. He would play a trick of his own and save his mother.

Carefully he groped his way out of the ruins and across the snowy courtyard. He hugged himself for warmth as he walked down the hill past the old houses. Instead of going back to the bridge, he turned east.

His mother's sister, Auntie Dawn, lived in a little village not far from town. He stumbled along the road. Fields lay on either side. Weeds stuck up through the fresh snow like whiskers. A breeze blew. Wisps of snow wriggled like snakes across the bare fields.

Little Lee reached his aunt's village at daybreak. The thatched roofs gleamed like gold beneath the rising sun. Somewhere in the village, a rooster crowed hoarsely. He kept it short as if he, too, felt the cold. Smoke was already rising cheerily from kitchen fires.

Little Lee picked up his feet. When he reached Auntie Dawn's house, he could hear her in the kitchen. Her pots and pans clattered industriously. He could smell something good inside.

When he knocked, she answered right away. Her cheeks were rosy from cooking. Auntie Dawn was astonished to see him. "Little Lee, what are you doing here? Come in."

Auntie Dawn ushered him into the kitchen where breakfast bubbled and sizzled. On one wall, nine foxtails hung from a nail. Uncle Smoky and his grown sons sat on benches at a table. Little Lee's cousins helped their father in his blacksmith shop. They were just as surprised at Little Lee's visit.

"What brings you here on a cold morning?" First Cousin asked.

Auntie Dawn frowned at her son. "You know your father always says food first. Talk later."

Uncle Smoky was a big bearded man of few words. He grunted in agreement.

"Our father also says that a mind always works better on a full belly," Second Cousin added.

Uncle Smoky grunted again.

First Cousin got up obligingly and poured Little Lee a cup of hot tea. Gratefully, Little Lee wrapped his hands around it and let the heat chase away the numbness. When he drank the tea, he felt its warmth fill him.

Second Cousin set a spoon and chopsticks before Little Lee. Third Cousin brought him a bowl of rice porridge. It was flavored with preserved eggs and dried onion.

Auntie Dawn served long, thin dough-nuts. Little Lee ate hungrily.

As she gave him another freshly fried doughnut, Auntie Dawn laughed. "Eat too fast and you'll get sick," she chuckled. Little Lee paused in embarrassment. Auntie Dawn patted him on the shoulder. "I was just joking. Eat, boy," she encouraged.

Little Lee did exactly that. He ate as much as Uncle Smoky and his grown sons. While

Little Lee ate, he listened to Auntie Dawn. She was humming the same tune Mama hummed when she had cooked.

Being around Auntie Dawn made Little Lee wish for the good old days before Father had left. It made him more determined than ever to carry out his plan.

Little Lee looked at the foxtails on the wall opposite to the stove and turned to Uncle Smoky. "Uncle," Little Lee asked, "how did you get the foxtails?"

"It was a very odd story," Auntie Dawn said from the stove. "Your uncle was in another town to repair the metal hinges of a set of gates. The job took so long that it was late at night before he finished." Auntie Dawn looked sternly over her shoulder. "He should have gone to an inn and slept there."

Uncle Smoky grinned contritely at his wife.

Auntie Dawn continued. "But he didn't want to worry me, so he started for home in the dark. As he passed by a grave mound, he saw a strange flickering light. Well, your uncle is the curious sort." She frowned at her husband.

Uncle Smoky smiled apologetically.

Auntie Dawn patted him on the shoulder. "He went to investigate. Next to a hole by the side of the mound, he saw a family of foxes. One fox had gold fur and nine tails. Now ghost foxes are shot so full of magic that they fairly crackle with it. In fact, if they just brush their tails against the ground, sparks will come out like fire. Well, this was one such fox. It was sitting up so it could hold the flames in its forepaws. As the ghost fox fanned the fire higher with its breath, it bragged about how it was going to burn down the town."

Uncle Smoky nodded his head in agreement.

"Well, your uncle doesn't stand for that sort of thing. He had his tools with him. He jumped into the foxhole and swung away." In her excitement, Auntie Dawn's long cooking chopsticks flailed at the air. "One blow, two, three. Uncle Smoky killed all those villains!"

Uncle Smoky pointed dramatically at the nine foxtails as Auntie Dawn continued. "He took the nine tails as proof. Tails for a tale, you see?"

As Auntie Dawn described Uncle Smoky's other adventures, Little Lee stared at the nine tails. It was just the thing he needed to rescue his mother.

When everyone could eat no more, Auntie Dawn stood behind her husband. "Your uncle has been hearing all sorts of rumors about you."

Uncle Smoky nodded his head silently.

Little Lee licked his lips. On his way to Auntie Dawn's house, he had figured out what to say. "It was all a misunderstanding. I wouldn't disobey my mother." That was true in a way—the woman in his house was not his mother.

He went on telling half-truths: "In fact, I came to help her. We have animals in the house. I think it might be rats. We could buy some poison in our own town, but then that old snoop, Auntie Spring, might find out. She'd spread the gossip all over town. So I snuck out early and came here."

Auntie Dawn seemed relieved. "Well, your uncle didn't believe those rumors for a moment. I'm sure your uncle will lend you some poison."

Uncle Smoky nodded his head and rose.

"Our father says it's time to go to work," one of his cousins said, and got up himself.

After they left for the smithy, Little Lee helped Auntie Dawn clear the dishes. When they were finished, he said, "May I have the poison now, Auntie?"

When Auntie Dawn left the room, Little Lee dragged a bench over to the wall and took down the foxtails. Quickly he hitched up his robe and tied the tails around his waist. He dragged the bench back to the table before Auntie Dawn returned with a small packet.

"Don't try to walk home in the snow," she said. "Keep me company. After work, your

uncle will ask a neighbor for a cart and take you."

To his relief, she did not notice the trophy was missing. Little Lee took the packet of poison. "That's very kind of you, Auntie. But mother's very upset about the rats. I think I should head home right away."

"Aren't you a good boy," Auntie Dawn said. "You deserve a reward, too." She went over to a pantry and got him a package of sweets.

Little Lee bowed his thanks and took the package of sweets. "I've only borrowed what I've taken," he said, meaning both the tails as well as the poison. "I'll return everything."

Then he left before Auntie Dawn could say another word.

10. The Market

LITTLE LEE stopped just outside Auntie Dawn's village. In his mind, he thanked Auntie Dawn again. He thought he was going to have to beg for candy in town, but Auntie Dawn had given him everything he needed.

Carefully he unwrapped the candy. Then he poured the powdered poison onto it. Wrapping it up again, he put it into his sleeve.

He readjusted the nine foxtails tied to his waist and set out again. By afternoon, he had returned to his town. Quickly he hurried through the streets to the broad, open square of the market.

Hens cackled in their cages. Pigs grunted at the ends of their ropes. Fishes and eels, fresh from the river, swam in the pails beneath the ice on the surface.

The stall keepers added to the noise as they shouted the virtues of their wares. They sold everything from dried turnips to toys and hats and candy. From the south, there were even bolts of silk spun by dragons.

Little Lee waited near the candy stall a long, anxious time. Finally he saw Brown Robe strolling toward the candy vendor. Quickly, Little Lee sidled up to him. "Excuse me," Little Lee said to Brown Robe. "Don't I know you from somewhere?"

Brown Robe stared at Little Lee suspicously. "I doubt it. I'm from North Village. Where do you live?"

Little Lee knew he would scare Brown Robe away if he was too pushy. He had to pretend to be a ghost fox who was just as cautious, too. Glancing around he lowered his voice so that only Brown Robe could hear him. He hinted that he wasn't human, but a fox who lived in a cave. "I live in a place called Hillside—in a cozy little cave."

Brown Robe jerked his head up in surprise, but he didn't say anything. Little Lee continued, "My family's lived there for centuries. Hasn't yours?"

"I don't know what you mean," Brown Robe said carefully.

"Come now. I met your master in the garden behind the Ho family mansion." Little Lee nodded in the direction of the ruined mansion.

Still suspicious, Brown Robe studied him from head to toe. "You must be mistaken. No one lives in that old heap."

Little Lee glanced all around. When he was sure no one else was watching he raised the hem of his robe. Brown Robe could see the nine foxtails Little Lee had borrowed from Uncle Smoky. "We have to be careful what we take with us when we go shopping," Little Lee told Brown Robe.

When he saw the nine tails, Brown Robe thought Little Lee was a powerful ghost fox. "Great sir, you must forgive me. Your disguise is really too good. May I inquire your purpose in coming here?"

Little Lee dropped his hem and pointed toward the candy stall. "I had a taste for sweets. So I came to buy some."

"That's why I'm here, too," Brown Robe sighed. "But we're poor, so we have to steal what we want."

Little Lee frowned. "That's dangerous. What if they catch you?"

Brown Robe spread out his hands helplessly. "When a master orders, a servant obeys. Unfortunately my master loves sweets so much that I've stolen from the candy seller too much. I'm sure she suspects me by now."

Little Lee deliberated for a moment. "It's better to buy than to steal. Why don't you take mine?" He slipped the package of candy from his sleeve. "I've got plenty of money in my purse, and I can always buy more."

Brown Robe was so relieved and grateful that he did not know what to say at first.

Little Lee pressed the package into his hands. "We belong to the same family in the end." He winked meaningfully at his pun.

"It's always risky to steal," Brown Robe agreed and took the candy with many thank-yous.

Little Lee watched him leave the market and walk toward the Ho family mansion. Then Little Lee returned home.

11. The Hero

THAT NIGHT, while his mother lay sick and unmoving in her room, Little Lee went to the kitchen and got a knife. Then he sat down outside his mother's door. However, Red Robe did not come, and his mother slept peacefully through the next morning.

When Auntie Dawn and Uncle Smoky came to visit that day, Little Lee peeked inside her room.

Mama was awake. "What strange, terrible dreams I've been having. I felt as if I were drowning." Mama smiled at him weakly.

"But I feel as if I've risen from the bottom of the river."

Little Lee gave her a hug. "And I felt as if I had to go there to find you."

His mother suddenly looked anxious. "I did such terrible things to you in the dreams."

Little Lee held onto her as if he would never let her go. "You're back with me now."

"But how?" his mother asked.

"It's easier to show you," Little Lee said. He ushered Auntie Dawn and Uncle Smoky into his mother's room to keep her company. Then he went to his room and got the nine foxtails.

When he returned, he presented the tails to Auntie Dawn. "These belong to you. Please forgive me for borrowing them without asking first."

Auntie Dawn scratched her head. "Your uncle was wondering where his trophy went."

Uncle Smoky nodded his head in agreement.

So Little Lee told them his story. However, when he was finished, Auntie Dawn took his pulse. "I think the boy's touched."

"Everything I said is true," Little Lee insisted. "If you go with me to the Ho mansion, you'll see for yourselves."

Uncle Smoky motioned for them to wait there. He returned with a sedan chair for Little Lee's mother. When she was comfortable inside, Little Lee set off. The chair followed him while Little Lee's uncle and aunt kept pace on either side.

A thaw had melted the snow, but the mud had frozen. Though it was very slippery, Little Lee led them to the Ho mansion and around to the garden. There, under the plum trees, two foxes lay dead. One had red fur, and the other had brown. A bandage was still tied around the tail of the red fox. Between them lay a package of candy.

Auntie Dawn recognized the wrapping. "Isn't that the candy I gave you?"

Little Lee clasped his hands behind his back. "Yes, it's just as I said."

Uncle Smoky carried the ghost foxes back down to their house and showed them to their neighbors. Suddenly the very same people who had scolded Little Lee now gushed over his goodness and cleverness. Auntie Spring was the loudest. "He's a saint, a saint. I knew it all the time. Didn't I tell everyone?"

But Little Lee ignored her praise. He was relieved that he had saved his mother from the ghost foxes. And now they could renew their walks down to the river, just like the good old days.

12. Homecoming

AND on New Year's Eve, when the plum blossoms had fallen like snow, they saw his father's boat. It seemed to crawl up the river. His father and the crew used long poles to shove it along. Big Lee had kept his promise, just as Little Lee had kept his.

From the deck, his father waved to them. From the shore, Little Lee and his mother waved back.